THE ROCKER CHICK HALL OF FAME

YOUR PICTURE HERE.

THINK YOU CAN HANDLE
JAMIE KELLY'S FIRST YEAR OF DIARIES?

AND DON'T MISS YEAR TWO!

DEAR DUMB DIARY,

THAT'S WHAT FRIENDS AREN'T FOR

BY JAMIE KELLY

SCHOLASTIC INC.

No part of this publication may be reproduced, stored in a retrieval system, or transmitted in any form or by any means, electronic, mechanical, photocopying, recording, or otherwise, without written permission of the publisher. For information regarding permission, write to Scholastic Inc., Attention: Permissions Department, 557 Broadway, New York, NY 10012.

ISBN 978-0-545-11612-1

20 19 18 17 16 15 14 16 17 18 19 20 /0

Printed in the U.S.A.   40

First printing, January 2010

For my dad, Robert Daniel Benton

Thanks to my BFFs at Scholastic:
Steve Scott, Cheryl Weisman,
Susan Jeffers Casel, Anna Bloom,
and BBFF Shannon Penney.

And special thanks to BWF Mary K.,
and BNF Kristen Leclerc.

This Diary
Property
of

Jamie Kelly

SCHOOL: *Mackerel Middle School*

BEST FRIEND: Isabella, who I **CHOSE** as a friend and who wasn't **JAMMED** down my throat.

FAVORITE MONSTER: probably a werewolf because it's closest to a Yorkshire Terrier.

HOW TO TELL IF somebody is your friend: You can't.

AND if you're **NOT** my friend...

guess WHAT?

BOOM! Now you ARE!

so STOP READING THIS!

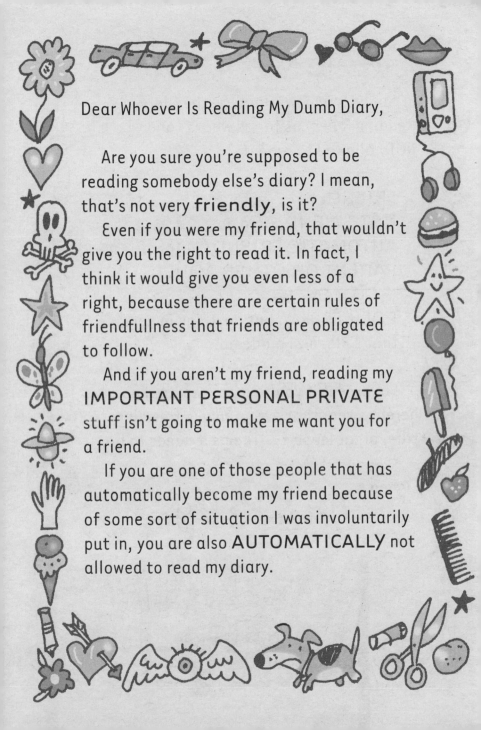

Dear Whoever Is Reading My Dumb Diary,

Are you sure you're supposed to be reading somebody else's diary? I mean, that's not very **friendly**, is it?

Even if you were my friend, that wouldn't give you the right to read it. In fact, I think it would give you even less of a right, because there are certain rules of friendfullness that friends are obligated to follow.

And if you aren't my friend, reading my **IMPORTANT PERSONAL PRIVATE** stuff isn't going to make me want you for a friend.

If you are one of those people that has automatically become my friend because of some sort of situation I was involuntarily put in, you are also **AUTOMATICALLY** not allowed to read my diary.

So, let's review. Here are the Diary Reading Rules, as far as who is (and who is NOT) allowed to read it:

FRIEND: No.
NOT FRIEND: Also no.
AUTOMATIC FRIEND: Automatic no.
PARENT OR OTHER ADULT CITIZEN: No.
POLICE: OKAY, but anything in here that's illegal, I made up.

So, except if you're a policeman, I do hereby swear that everything in this diary is true, or, at least, as true as it needs to be.

Signed,

Jamie Kelly

Sunday 01

Dear Dumb Diary,

You know how in movies when people are in love they kiss like they're trying to get something that's stuck in each other's teeth? My dog Stinker has this toy he likes to kiss passionately like that. Or maybe he's chewing it, I don't know. It's hard to tell. There's a lot of **mouth action** and some obvious deep feelings.

Movie people manage to keep the foam to a minimum during these scenes, a policy that is not shared by Stinker. It's probably because those actors are just *pretending* to care about each other. Stinker's gross devotion is sincere.

I call this toy of his **Grossnasty**. None of us know what it was when it started out — could have been a teddy bear, could have been a pair of undies. But anything that a beagle **Loves Up** this much for years and years takes on an appearance that can't be understood by the human brain. Such is the power of Beagle Froth.

Recently, when the wet, slobbery chewing sound and dog-saliva odor became too much for me to endure, I decided to throw Grossnasty away. I walked right up to Stinker with a trash can, stooped down, and touched the horrid toy by its ear or waistband or whatever.

YOINK

And Stinker **EXPLODED** into this snapping, growling, spitty ball of fury that actually scared me enough to make me jump up on my dresser. (He looked just like the werewolf in that one werewolf movie I totally want to see.)

Fortunately, I maintain a very cluttered room, and I had numerous knickknacks within reach to hurl at him until he backed down. If my room had been as tidy as my mom wants it, there is a very good chance that I would have been swallowed by an enraged beagle.

People. For safety's sake, KEEP A MESSY ROOM.

In addition to old fat beagle Stinker, we now also own his **dogdaughter**, Stinkette, who we got by means of Stinker's unapproved marriage to Angeline's dog, Stickybuns. (Why am I telling you all this again, Diary? You remember this, don't you?)

Back to Stinkette: This morning, Stinkette stupidly waddled up to Stinker — who was really going to town on his beloved Grossnasty — and she chomped down on it and tugged.

I instantly leaped up on my dresser with a ceramic bear bank aimed directly at Stinker's fangs. I was ready for him to launch into fat werewolf-dog mode, but he did . . . nothing.

In fact, he even wagged his tail a little. (He never wags his tail, so it cracked like a bunch of old knuckles.) Then Stinkette pulled Grossnasty away from him, hopped up on my bed, and started to grossfully chew on it herself. Stinker actually *gave his dogdaughter the single item he loved most in the whole world*. Something suddenly became very clear to me: *I really want to burn that bedspread now.*

Also: *Stinker is a bigger dope than I thought.*

Oops. Just remembered I was supposed to call Isabella to come over and study math today. She's afraid she might fail and have to take summer school.

It's not like I can help her very much. I'm just not very good at math. It always seems so cold and unemotional to me.

The teacher says that **Two** plus **Three** equals **Five**, but nobody asked the poor little number **Two** if she even wanted to get added up with **Three**, and now that **Two** and **Three** equaled **Five** together, are they supposed to be lifelong friends or something? Just because some mathematician said so? And maybe it's just me, but **Seven** always looks like he's up to no good.

I hate math.

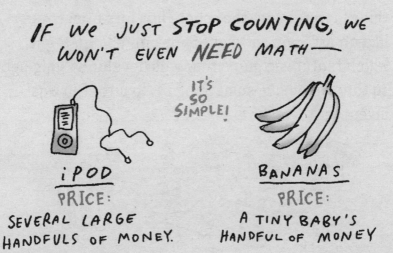

IF WE JUST STOP COUNTING, WE WON'T EVEN NEED MATH—

IT'S SO SIMPLE!

iPOD
PRICE:
SEVERAL LARGE HANDFULS OF MONEY.

BANANAS
PRICE:
A TINY BABY'S HANDFUL OF MONEY

Monday 02

Dear Dumb Diary,

We've entered that part of the school year where you begin to wonder if maybe even the teachers are beginning to lose interest in education. We study something — like igneous rocks, or spit molecules, or one of those countries that looks like where they are going to build a country one day — we glue-stick a bunch of things about it to a piece of poster board, they get hung up in the hallway, and then we never talk about them again.

So toward the end of the year, just to keep things interesting, the school has lots of events like an Art Show, a Talent Show, and Bingo Night, which features a game that was developed long ago so that we'd have something to do until fun was invented.

If I ever become a teacher, I'm going to jazz it up a bit. Maybe I'll glue-stick the **actual students** up in the hallway, and when you walk up to one, he'll have to tell you what he knows about spit molecules or whatever.

Also, I'm going to make it so that if a kid bothers me, I can legally shoot her out of a cannon. I really may have **psychic powers**, because I think I've read the mind of a teacher who was thinking that exact thing one time when Mike Pinsetti got almost all of a crayon stuck in his ear.

And speaking of shooting somebody out of a cannon, I don't know if I've ever mentioned this girl to you before, Diary — her name is Angeline?

First, before we discuss Angeline, let's take a moment to discuss **AUTOMATIC FRIENDSHIPS**. Automatic Friendships occur like this: Let's say you and a person from your school who you only *kind of know* both show up at the same beach one day and there's nobody else to hang around with. BAM — you're *Automatic Friends*. Maybe only for a day, but still. It's just the Way the Universe Does Things.

Doesn't matter who— For that day You're AUTOMATIC FRIENDS

Or let's say you go to prison. You committed some cool crime like stealing the weapon of somebody who was going to blast an endangered baby orphan koala in the face. Still, the judge says that **stealing is stealing**, and he sends you to prison for it. And in prison, you meet somebody who is in for the same kind of crime, but for her it was like an endangered baby orphan panda or just an endangered baby orphan. BAZOOM — now you two are *Automatic* Friends.

Ever since Angeline's Uncle Dan (my school's assistant principal) married my Aunt Carol, and Angeline's dog married my dog and they had puppies together, I'm *automatically* friends with Angeline. No beach, no orphan koalas, just KABLAM — Automatic Friends.

You'll notice that it's not because I like her. It's just how things work. It's like math: Poor little **Two** got plussed with **Three**.

So now I'm friends with Angeline. This is an **Automatic Friendship**, and I have to just accept it and make the best of things.

See, if I objected, then Aunt Carol might divorce Angeline's uncle, sending both of them tumbling into a deep pit of depression for the rest of their lives, and Angeline could wind up feeling so guilty that she would have to go be locked up in an old dirty insane asylum for years and years, and Stinker's puppies would grow up not knowing both their parents — and I couldn't live with myself for doing something like that to a puppy.

I've talked to Isabella about the Angeline thing, since she's my BFF. That's what best friends are for, after all. But she seems to think that we should be friends with Angeline, and that if I'm having a problem with Angeline, we should just hug it out.

You know, maybe that *would* help. When you think about it, choking is just a hug that your hands give to a throat.

Isabella says that Angeline thinks of the three of us like BFFs. I could have pointed out to Isabella that, last time I counted, there are only two *Fs* in BFF. And there's a reason for that. If you get too many *Fs*, it doesn't look like *Best Friends Forever* anymore. It looks like you're trying to spell the sound a fart makes. Observe: BFFFFFFFFFFFFF.

But I didn't say that, because we're all automatically such terribly good friends now. Terribly, terribly good friends. **Terribly, terribly.**

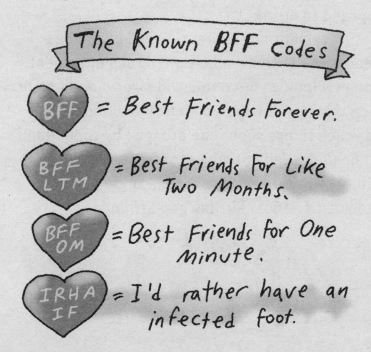

The Known BFF Codes

BFF = Best Friends Forever.

BFF LTM = Best Friends For Like Two Months.

BFF OM = Best Friends for One Minute.

IRHA IF = I'd rather have an infected foot.

Tuesday 03

Dear Dumb Diary,

When I got to school today, Angeline was standing at Isabella's locker and the two of them were talking about something that was making Angeline laugh and laugh. This would have bothered somebody who is not friends with Angeline but since we're all terribly good pals now, I guess it was really great. Or whatever the word is for something that is supposed to be great.

Sure, morning locker time USED to be a Jamie-Isabella thing, where we'd take a moment to quietly look at the Whole Wide World and decide which things in it were wonderful and beautiful and which things should be dragged by their blond hair behind a cement mixer for five miles. But that was way back before Angeline and I became Automatic Friends. Terribly good friends.

Attach here

Okay. We're friends now. Remember how I said that already? How many times do I have to say it?

Back to the lockers: As I got a little closer, I could see what they were laughing at. Way off in the distance, six lockers down, Hudson Rivers (eighth cutest boy in my grade) was trying to secretly get a look at Isabella through the odor vents of another kid's locker. It's romantic, of course, but the vents are angled and it's hard to see through them. Plus, he wasn't really doing a very good job of hiding.

We recently learned that Hudson has some sort of ridiculous crush on Isabella instead of the ridiculous one he used to have on Angeline or the meaningful one he had on me. So I guess it was pretty funny, although it's kind of tragic in a way, since Isabella wouldn't give him the time of day.

I'm not kidding: The other day, he asked her what time it was and she said, "I won't tell you."

I helped Isabella laugh at Hudson (I mean, what are friends for?), and I was even friendly to Angeline by saying a really friendly sentence like, "Hello."

Long ago, I might have thought of using a sentence with the term **"donkey butt"** in it. But not anymore. That is really quite friendly of me.

I do wonder how Angeline feels now that Hudson is all **gaga** over Isabella. Poor Angeline just can't bring the cute the way she used to. I guess maybe cute-bringing takes its toll.

Not calling people "ANIMAL BUTTS."

more PROOF of HOW SUPER Nice I am!!!

The rest of today went pretty much like all Tuesdays go: The thrill of the weekend is behind you, but the crushing resentment of Wednesday has not begun.

Tuesdays are how I imagine being an adult will feel *every day*. Except when I get to be as old as my parents. Then I think it will always feel like Monday morning. In February. And it's snowing polar bears. And they have rabies.

Oh — I got a new reading assignment today. We're supposed to select a "classic" book to read, and by "classic," they mean "old."

I love to read, but I don't want a book with a bunch of "thees" and "thous" and "thines" in it. Can you imagine how excited the **old-timey people** were when somebody invented "you" and "your" to use instead? It probably meant that they could take their old-timey leotards off as well.

Let's lose these stupid COLLARS, too.

I'm going to show the list of books to my parents and let them make a suggestion. I'm sure they know all the classic books on the list, since they're both really **"classic"** themselves. They're always doing something classic, like when my mom grunts when she stands up. My dad is so classic that he has hair growing out of his classic ears.

How to Tell if Somebody is "Classic"

THEIR DIET HAS A LOT OF FIBER FOCUS

BRAN COOKIES

BRAN SODA

PURE BRAN WITH BRAN LUMPS

THEIR MEDICINE CABINET CONTAINS MOSTLY MEDICINE.

EYE MED

GROUCH PILLS

BIFOCAL OINTMENT

THEY WOULD FEEL SLIGHTLY INSULTED IF THEY READ THIS.

THAT'S DISRESPECTFUL

Wednesday 04

Dear Dumb Diary,

HOORAY!! In art class today, Miss Anderson (who is pretty enough to be a hairstylist but settled for teacher instead) announced the SCHOOL ART SHOW.

The Art Show is a big deal at Mackerel Middle School — if your work is chosen, it gets framed and hung up, and they put up an official card with your name underneath it, and then they have a party with refreshments. They even put an ad in the paper to let people know about the show. The parents all come and look at the stuff on the walls and lie to you that yours is the best. Except my parents, who don't lie when they tell me mine is the best.

No event is official without refreshments.

As you know, Dumb Diary, I love to draw, and one of my artworks has won an award at the Art Show every year since I first entered way back in second grade.

For some reason, back then I was obsessed with drawing naked Barbies. The teachers didn't feel that those were appropriate for a kids' art show, so they used the only artwork I did all year without a naked Barbie in it, which was this picture of a cow in front of a barn. It really wasn't a very good drawing, but I thought it was cool because I made it out of cut-up construction paper and the doors of the barn could open.

At the Art Show, I discovered that they had neglected to open the doors on my little barn, so I opened them myself, which revealed the dozen little naked Barbies within. I won a prize right then and there, because they felt they needed to use the third-place ribbon to quickly **seal the doors closed**, probably for eternity.

SLAM!

This year's big Art Show isn't for a month, but I'm planning on starting early. A masterpiece could take days to complete, and I really want my new friend Angeline to be **terribly, terribly proud** of how excellent her friend Jamie is at art, in spite of the fact that Angeline couldn't draw flies even if she was covered in manure.

WAIT. That was not a friendly thing to say. Let me try again, as a friend: I would really and truly encourage Angeline not to give up, and motivate her to keep working at it, and **eventually** I'm sure she could draw those flies.

Saying It In A Friendly Way

NOT FRIENDLY	♥ FRIENDLY ✎
"She's mean."	"She's good at being in charge."
"He's dumb."	"He's fun to play word games with."
"You're fat."	"You're Gravity's favorite!"

Thursday 05

Dear Dumb Diary,

    Thursday is Meat Loaf Day. Did you ever wonder how they make meat loaf, Dumb Diary? It's really fascinating. Here's what they do:
1. Start out with a big lump of meat, probably from some kind of an animal.
2. Run it though a grinder.
3. Bake it back into a big lump of meat.

    Miss Bruntford, the cafeteria monitor, used to hassle us all the time to finish the meat loaf because she hated us so much. But now she's friends with Aunt Carol, so she hassles us to finish it because she cares about us so much. Either way, it winds up with me trying to squeeze down a plate full of horse meat once a week.

There's probably a place where they raise animals in loaf form.

In between today's lunchtime gag reflexes, Isabella showed me a poster she had torn down announcing the School Talent Show. Isabella thought it would be cool to enter, and when I asked her what she thought we could do, she got this weird look on her face.

My psychic powers told me that she was thinking something like: **What do you mean "WE"?** Plus, my ear powers were telling me the exact same thing at the exact same moment, because that's what she actually said.

School teaches you how to have polite conversations while you try not to HORK up your lunch.

See, Isabella actually does have a talent all her own. She does magic. I was right there when she discovered her love of it for the very first time. We were at my house watching TV, and this magician came on and sawed a lady in half. Isabella got hysterically happy and said, "Do you think they'd let him do that to *anybody*? Could he do that to his brothers?"

The fact that the magician restored the lady at the end made no impression on Isabella. "He didn't *have* to put her back together," she said.

As time went on, Isabella learned that the whole **cutting-a-person-in-half** thing was just a trick, but she has a natural fondness for deceiving people, and she's not even bothered by the nerd factor that comes with doing magic. And the fact that magic will probably never be her job doesn't bother her, either. For Isabella, the mere joy of making people look like idiots is reward enough.

"You're thinking about doing a magic act, right?" I said.

And Isabella just said, "Maybe."

"Well, maybe I could help you," I said.

And Isabella just said, "Maybe."

"Magicians need beautiful assistants," I said, "and I could do that."

Isabella said, "You know, an assistant could be a good idea."

And then, right in the middle of a private conversation, Angeline (who was probably bred by scientists with the exact physical requirements to be a **Professional Magician's Assistant**) flopped down in a chair, distracting me and Isabella and everybody at the table — which is the EXACT THING a magician's assistant is *supposed* to do to the audience — and said, "Have you guys heard about the Talent Show?"

"Have you ever seen a magic act?" Isabella asked her right away. "You know how they have assistants? Like, blond assistants?"

The conversation didn't go any further, partly because the bell rang, but mostly because I grabbed Isabella's backpack and she had to chase me down to get it. I shouldn't have done it, but I just don't want Isabella to do the Talent Show without me, even though I know it would be perfect for her and Angeline to go and do the Talent Show together.

I mean it would be *totally* perfect. Just **PERFECTLY PERFECT**. So terribly, terribly, terribly perfect. It really shouldn't bother me if I'm left out of that, right? It's no big deal, right?

So what if I'm not in the Talent Show with my BFF and we don't have our morning locker time to be mean to people anymore? I can live with that, right?

It's not like I should tear blond handfuls of somebody's blond hair out of their blond skull, right?

see, this might be wrong.

Friday 06

Dear Dumb Diary,

   Aunt Carol called to invite me to a movie tonight, because she is the awesomest aunt **In The History of Ever**, and she knew that I really, really wanted to see this movie about a werewolf that falls in love with this girl and then a tragic thing happens or something. I don't know, I only saw the commercial. But Aunt Carol knew I wanted to go, and to show that her awesomeness is even awesomer than awesome, she also invited Isabella to go with us.

if your boyfriend is a werewolf you Automatically get a Dog, too.

I was getting ready for the movie and pulling on my sock, but it must have shrunk because it was really hard to get on, and so I was hopping around on one foot when Aunt Carol pulled up. Out my bedroom window, I saw Aunt Carol and Isabella get out of the car . . . followed by Angeline, who my Aunt Carol must have invited since we're automatically friends now. **Isn't. That. Great.**

I was still bouncing around trying to pull my sock on, when the **PURE JOY** at seeing that Angeline was going to the movies with us made me slip and fall. Fortunately, I fell on my soft, cushy bed.

BOUNCE
BOUNCE
BOUNCE

Unfortunately, my bed is exactly where Stinkette had recently been furiously slobbering all over Grossnasty. As I fell, my mouth open in scream-position, a large portion of the Heinous Object **ENTERED MY MOUTH DEEP ENOUGH FOR ME TO EAT IT.**

(DRAWN IN SLOW MOTION)

Through my horror, I could hear Aunt Carol and my mom yelling for me to hurry up or we're going to miss the movie, and then Angeline yelled up an apology for getting the movie time wrong. So that's why I had to hurry like crazy and not stop to give my mouth the three-hour toothbrushing it required. Don't worry — I didn't actually eat Grossnasty, but it was fully, almost completely in my mouth and that was bad enough.

I didn't have any gum or mints and I was in a big hurry, and so all I could do was grab a tube of toothpaste and stick it in my pocket. I figured I could just get some of it in my mouth secretly.

I kept gagging a little all the way to the theater, on account of having a mouthful of dog-saliva flavor, but I smiled prettily through it all because of my intense acting abilities.

When we got to the theater there was no time to stop at the concession stand. The movie was packed, so I had to sit right next to a little girl who was at least two full years younger than me, and therefore **MUCH TOO YOUNG** to see a movie with werewolves in it. **MUCH, MUCH, MUCH TOO YOUNG.**

I just can't emphasize enough that the little girl's mom should have known that a werewolf movie could be **TOO FRIGHTENING** to take a little girl to.

The movie might have been great, I don't really know. I was focused on the horrible taste in my mouth. Every time I tried to secretly get the toothpaste up to my mouth, the little girl next to me would notice that I was doing something, and she would look over and smile at me. So, being a super-friendly person, I smiled back.

Finally, the movie came to a really scary part — so scary that when I tried again to get the toothpaste to my mouth, the little girl, horrified by the werewolf on screen, didn't look over at me, and I finally delivered a big gush of toothpaste to my yucky mouth.

Maybe **TOO** big of a gush.

So then I had a huge mouthful of toothpaste. I swear, toothpaste really seems to get bigger in your mouth, and you can't swallow it, so it just sits in there getting foamier and foamier.

This time, when the little girl looked over, it wasn't because she saw me doing something. It was because she was petrified. And me, being friendly, did what I had been doing all night: **I smiled at her**.

Okay. Let me just say, for the record, that I look nothing like a werewolf. Nobody could ever mistake me for one.

Except maybe if they were really young, and it was really dark, and they were watching a scary werewolf movie and I smiled at them with a mouthful of **dripping, frothy slobber**.

Aunt Carol calmed down by the time we got home. As many times as I told her that I hadn't tried to scare that little girl on purpose, I don't think she ever really believed me. I didn't want to admit that I had mouthed Grossnasty, so having the toothpaste with me was impossible to explain.

It was the first time Aunt Carol had ever been that mad at me, and the first time any of us had been asked to leave a movie theater. Except for Isabella, of course, who has been asked to leave most places.

Not that I can blame this on anybody. I mean, I guess if Angeline hadn't shown up in the car and startled me I wouldn't have mouthed Grossnasty, and if she hadn't read the movie time wrong I would have had time to brush my teeth at home, and if her dog hadn't married Stinker then Stinkette wouldn't be around to leave Grossnasty on my bed in the first place, but you can hardly blame my terribly good Automatic Sisterfriend for any of that, right?

A few other places Isabella has been asked to leave...

The Grocery Store

Her own Baptism

Some countries

Saturday 07

Dear Dumb Diary,

I tried having some talent today.

I'm just not going to let this go. I have to come up with something that Isabella and I can do together in the Talent Show. Otherwise, I'm going to be sitting unhappily in the audience watching the Isabella and Angeline Show. Which would be perfect for them, but every now and then I also have to think of myself.

I'm a really good dancer. I mean, everybody knows that. It's been said that my moves are **funktastic** — and not by just anybody, but by those who know their funky. But Isabella can't dance. Or won't. I've never figured out which. It's one of **Isabella's Great Mysteries.**

CRACK
CRACK
CRACK
CRACK

Also she can crack every joint in her body including her tongue.

I'm really good at acting and drama stuff, too. In fact, I'm so good I pronounce it *"duh-rama"* because it sounds more dramatic that way. Isabella has spent her whole life perfecting only fake-crying in order to get her mean older brothers in trouble, so if a role were to call for anything else, like **Delicate Sweetness** (a specialty of mine), *duh-rama* would become impossible for her.

More of my Duh-rama specialties

Delicate Sadness

ADORABLY CRAZY

Charming Screamfulness

Farty but forgivable

I tried singing, and I thought I sounded pretty good until Stinker bit me a little for it. I had to admit that if somebody bites you for singing, you're doing it wrong. (It's really one of the main ways to know.)

Ventriloquism seems sort of like evil ghostly possession to me, which I oppose, and I don't want to juggle or twirl a baton. I'm not even sure baton twirling is a talent, exactly. You're really just playing a showy game of catch with yourself in an adorable sparkly outfit, and I think that makes it less of a talent and more of a sport that guys won't play.

The VENTRILOQUIST DUMMY— EVEN EVILER THAN MARIONETTES.

I ran out of talent ideas, so I went downstairs and flipped on the TV because TV doesn't really demand that you have any ideas. But right there on the TV, I saw this show with this band and it was made up entirely of girls.

Not only that, but they also solved mysteries, and went shopping for guitars and stuff, and looked really fashionable doing it. **It was like a miracle.** TV was actually telling me something useful.

TV was telling me that for the Talent Show, I needed to **Form a Band**. Thanks, TV!

Then it told me that our kitchen floor looked dingy and that I had to try this new gum. TV is smart, but it has a hard time staying on topic, kind of like that one kid at school who screams if anybody touches his locker.

ALSO, TV WAAAAY OVERESTIMATES HOW FUN SNACKS ARE TO US.

Sunday 08

Dear Dumb Diary,

    I showed my dad the list of classic books we had to pick from for school. He made me think of the list because he was taking a nap in the middle of the day on the couch **like a classic person**.
    He hadn't read all of them, but he said he really liked the movie *The Three Musketeers*, so maybe that book would be a good choice.

DAD LOOKING PRETTY CLASSIC

CLASSIC DAD SLOBBER

CLASSIC DAD SWEATPANTS

Dad told me that *The Three Musketeers* are these French guys with fancy hats and swords that save the day or something. Mom joined in and said it might be a good book for me because Isabella, Angeline, and I are like three musketeers. The thought of slashing swords around with those two both **delighted** and **terrified** me.

But then Dad added that *The Three Musketeers* were more like four musketeers, because a lot of the story revolves around a fourth guy that kind of joins up with the first three. He said that the fourth guy really made them complete, and even saved their lives from a shark. But then he said the shark might have been in another movie he saw, so it's hard to tell just how much of any of this he had right. And then he went back to sleep on the couch. (Looks like screamy kid and TV aren't the only ones with attention-span issues.)

OH DAD

But my dad's pointless jabbering made me think of something: The band I saw on TV had **four** people in it. That goes for most other bands, too.

And it's not just bands, either. Tennis never has three on a team. Ping-Pong never has three on a team. Crime-fighting superheroes never work in threes. You never see, like, Batman and Robin and Steve. You just know that Steve would get in the way and be all like, "Hey, what's this thing do? Can I drive the Batmobile? Maybe the Joker isn't such a bad guy — did you ever try to get to know him? HI, JOKER! WE'RE OVER HERE!"

I think I know what I must do.

I have a plan.

Like most plans, it has two phases. **Phase One**, or outer phase, which is like the frosting, and **Phase Two**, which is the inner phase, like the cake. That reminds me — I didn't do math homework with Isabella like she wanted. It might seem strange that this made me think of Isabella, but experience has taught me that wheresoever there is frosting, soon shall there also be Isabella.

Monday 09

Dear Dumb Diary,

Today I dropped the idea on Isabella of forming a band for the Talent Show. She didn't hate it. And that was a **critical moment** in my plan.

I even said we should include Angeline because my psychic powers told me that if I didn't, they might go and do Isabella's magic act without me, which Isabella said out loud at the exact same time as my powers said it.

(Honestly. My psychic powers would be a lot more impressive if people would allow enough time for them to occur before they said things.)

STOP doing things before I predict them, thank you

Handling Isabella is like handling a rattlesnake. Except that a real rattlesnake won't explode when you least expect it and blurt out some sort of embarrassing thing that it knows you did, like kissing a magazine cover until you got printer's ink all over your lips and you had to use dishwashing liquid to get it off. Not that I ever did that. Or ever will again.

Also, a rattlesnake won't sit on you and let just a little drool dribble out of its mouth and then suck it back up at the last moment. It's weird to think that my BFF has done things to me that are beneath a rattlesnake.

Anyway, handling Isabella is tricky, and nobody but me has even the slightest hope of doing it. **Observe:**

"But," I went on, "you might rather do the magic act. Magic is cool," I said. "Probably the coolest."

That was the bait. I crossed my fingers and waited.

I have sort of pretty hands.

"It's not the coolest," Isabella said. I knew that her undeniable expertness on coolness would come through. "A band *would* be the coolest."

"But you and I can't play anything," I said, crossing my fingers even harder. I tried crossing my toes. I think I may have crossed my organs. If the rattlesnake was going to explode, or sit on me and drool, this was the moment.

And that's where I left it. A less experienced Isabella-Handler might try to close the deal right then and there, but you have to be patient. If you try too hard to sell Isabella on something, she starts to get suspicious and might make you eat it without even taking it out of the box, like I've seen her do to Girl Scouts trying a little too hard to sell her cookies, and once with a second grader selling stuff for a class fund-raiser. (**Science Note:** you can get a roll of wrapping paper about a foot deep into a kid's mouth.)

Don't worry. I got it out mostly.

By lunchtime, I saw that Phase One (the frosting phase) was complete. Isabella was telling Angeline about our band as if it had been her idea all along. Angeline, being profoundly crippled with **Permanent Good Attitude**, is unable to respond to any idea in any way other than positively.

"We'll just pretend to play the instruments. And we'll pretend to sing. You know, like lip-synching," Isabella explained.

"That will be so funny!" Angeline said.

I saw the whole plan begin to crumble. FUNNY was not going to work for Isabella, and Angeline knew it.

I had to think fast. "You bet it will be funny," I said. "We'll fool everybody into thinking it's us playing and singing. We'll totally trick everybody. You're right, Angeline — funny." Then I said it again all stretched out: "FUUUUUUUUUUUUUUUUUUUUH-NEE."

I could have gone longer than that, but was worried that if I stretched out my UUUH a few *U*s too many, Isabella would know I was up to something. She can be very perceptive when it comes to **trickery**.

In that moment, I can imagine what was going on in Angeline's head. Part of her head wanted to object to the trickery of it. The rest of her head was devoted to full-time hair manufacturing. But another part, a **beensy-teensy** part of her head, really *liked* the idea of being up onstage as part of a band. What's cooler than people thinking you can rock out on a guitar?

"Yeah," she finally said. "Funny."

"Yeah," Isabella said. "Everyone will be totally fooled."

"Yeah," I said in an extremely casual and offhand kind of way. "Now I'll have some auditions for another band member."

FAKE COOL is almost as cool as REAL COOL.

"Another band member?" Isabella repeated, narrowing her eyes at me. I swear I heard a **rattlesnake ticking**.

Leave it to Angeline to play snake charmer. I guess Blondy bought the whole idea. "Makes sense to me," Angeline said. "It will look more like a real band with more performers."

Looking more like a real band meant fooling more people. This clearly pleased Isabella's wicked side, which is pretty much both her sides.

She nodded, and now Phase Two (the cake phase) was in motion.

HER WICKED SIDE ↓

HER OTHER WICKED SIDE ↓

ALSO HER MIDDLE IS A LITTLE WICKED ←

Hudson has been watching Isabella
ALL WEEK

Like a leopard
stalking an impala...

Like a shark
stalking a tuna...

Like a clown stalking cotton
candy or human souls or
whatever it is they eat.

Tuesday 10

Dear Dumb Diary,

I posted some flyers for band auditions today. Even with the handicap of not having glitter on them, I'm pretty sure they'll work. I couldn't really write **GIRLS ONLY** on the flyers, because I think it would be wrong to discriminate against the boy species without doing it secretly. So they say things like, "Fashion sense a must" and "High heel skills a plus" and "Should be able to sing prettily in a very high pretty voice."

Glitter would have helped the flyers, of course — there are few things it doesn't help — but I needed to save my full glitter assortment for my art project.

When I got home from school today, I spent several hours deciding what kind of art masterpiece I wanted to create. I was so happy to have put my Talent Show plan in motion that I just **arted all over the place.**

Even the combined repulsiveness of Stinker and his dogdaughter didn't distract me. They seemed content to sit there and watch me work and smell bad.

You understand, of course, that I meant that *they* smell bad, not me. I smell delicious: like glitter and a plan coming together.

ARTISTIC   ARTASTIC

Some Ideas I'm considering for my new Masterpiece...

"The koala fairy princess"

"The day the Aliens Abducted all the perfect girls"

"Biggest Glitter Speck ever."

"If the Moon had a nose it could smell my dogs right now."

Wednesday 11

Dear Dumb Diary,

Okay. See, if I owned the Universe — and maybe I should, I don't know, it's not up to me — when a person went to the bathroom, the rest of the Universe would politely wait until she got back before it did something stupid.

Today in art, Miss Anderson gave us one of her favorite assignments: Drawing portraits of each other during class. We were split up into pairs and had one class period to complete the portrait.

This is a classic art assignment of Miss Anderson's that helps us develop quick, confident drawing skills. It also permits Miss Anderson to talk to her new boyfriend on her cell phone for forty minutes. We've done this many, many times and everybody knows that Isabella and I **ALWAYS** pair up.

friendship necklace

You put peanut butter with jelly, bacon with eggs, and Jamie with Isabella. Nobody ever asks for a peanut butter and blond hair sandwich or a big plate of bacon and eggs and four-inch-long eyelashes.

I had to go to the bathroom **FOR, LIKE, ONE SECOND** and when I came back, Angeline **AND ISABELLA** had paired up for the portrait assignment. Just like that. Jelly with no peanut butter.

As I looked around, I realized that there was nobody left for me to pair up with except for **T.U.K.W.N.I.F.** (That Ugly Kid Whose Name I Forget). So now I was like one half of a peanut butter and sewage sandwich. Does that sound good to anybody? No? No takers?

It was even worse because I had to draw an ugly face. Sorry, T.U.K., I know it's not your fault, but it's not mine, either. Your parents are the ones that will do time for this crime.

I'm not saying that the parents of the ugly should be arrested.

Like everyone else, I'm whispering it.

Plus, as everybody knows, ol' T.U.K.ster can't draw portraits. Perhaps it's because he has grown up resenting faces, since his hasn't done him any favors. Maybe he's just all computery and not familiar with pencils and pencil-like-drawing-objects. Maybe because his face resembles so many other non-face things, he's a little unclear on exactly what role a face actually plays.

At the end of the class, Miss Anderson said we'd look at all of the portraits next week. She just picked up a couple portraits to show as examples to the class — T.U.K.W.N.I.F.'s and mine. My drawing of him was as flattering as I could possibly make it, and his drawing of me — which looked a lot like if an orangutan fell face-first into a blender — got a HUGE laugh.

Pretty Art teachers are good in case you need to Look At something Other THAN UGLY ART.

See, Universe, I'm not sure you got this one right. I think you really, really need to ask yourself if it was wise to make me and Isabella **AUTOMATIC** Friends with Angeline.

I think it may be time for me to admit that even though I've been trying very, very, very hard to make this whole three-way friendship with Isabella and Angeline and me work, I may have to let go of my dream and face the fact that Angeline is making me let go of my dream.

Three-person friendships are like three-person bands — they exist, but they're rare. Like unicorns and male librarians. (Which I believe were known in mythology as **Guybrarians**.)

other Mythological Creatures

HALF MAN, HALF BULL

HALF MAN, HALF ANT

HALF MAN, HALF SOME OTHER MAN.

Thursday 12

Dear Dumb Diary,

It's amazing, but I think my brain might have been trying to tell me something. You know, **like how TV does.**

Last night I had this dream —

Hey! It just occurred to me: Dreaming is just like watching TV, but you can't change the channel, and the shows often feature an insane clown that's trying to kill you. Or maybe that's just me.

Anyway, in this dream, Angeline and Isabella and I were all flowers. (Though Angeline might have been one of those weeds that looks like a flower.) We were just sitting there, growing, and my brain came walking along dressed up like an adorable little-girl gardener and planted a seed right next to us. The seed grew and grew into another flower, but I never saw its face.

Then this weasel-looking thing came along and said, "I'm hungry. I think I'll eat two scrumptious flowers." It bit the heads off of Angeline and the new flower. And Isabella and I were all laughing and high-fiving. Except that we had leaves for hands, so we were kind of high-oneing.

Do you see what this means, Dumb Diary? My brain is telling me that I need to get another friend, *not just another band member*. I need a *fourth friend* in our little group. Then Angeline will pair off with the new person, and Isabella and I can be the peanut butter and jelly that we're supposed to be.

IT'S SO SIMPLE. And here's how I'm going to do it: As girls audition to be our fourth band member for the talent show, they'll really be SECRETLY auditioning to be my new friend. And Isabella's friend and Angeline's friend, too, but I'll decide for all of us. I mean, that's what friends are for, right?

Secrets aren't
lies unless you
tell them.

Later in my flower dream, a bee came and stung me over and over in my flower face. I'm not sure what that means, but I put on a little bug spray this morning before I went to school. **Just in case.**

STAB
STABBY
STABBY

I don't think I like Nature very much anymore.

Today was Meat Loaf Day. Thursday is always Meat Loaf Day. So, to keep Miss Bruntford off my neck, I asked my mom to pack me a lunch. (If you bring your lunch from home, Miss Bruntford hardly even bothers you about what you're eating.)

Mom was flattered — and, let's face it, **kind of surprised** — that I asked. See, my mom's food is whatever that thing is just before it turns poisonous. Like, down at the government they can't really decide if her food should get that little skull-and-crossbones picture on it or not. Her food won't kill anybody most of the time, so maybe they'd give it a little skull-and-crossbones that's sort of hunching its shoulders in one of those "**I Don't Know**" gestures.

So, like I said, Mom was really flattered and spent a long time getting my lunch ready. I felt really good about how happy I had made her when I threw it all away.

THE WARNING ON KNOWN POISONS.

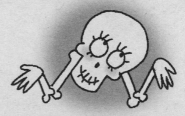

THE WARNING ON MOM'S FOOD.

I sat down with Isabella and Angeline and watched them eat and felt left out all over again because I sadly didn't have any lunch. I can't really say for sure whose fault that is. I imagined that I was a poor starving girl that, despite her extreme malnutrition, was very beautiful and had filth cutely smudged on her face just so.

Angeline tried to spoil my fantasy by offering me something from her lunch, but I didn't take it. We cutely unfortunate girls are too proud to accept charity and we don't really like raisins. I mean, if one day down at the raisin factory they accidentally dropped a bunch of dehydrated warts in your raisins, would you be able to tell?

Other Things You'd Never Be Able To Detect

A TOENAIL IN YOUR CORNFLAKES

OLD PERSON EYEBROW HAIR IN YOUR TOOTHBRUSH

SLEEPING GAS IN MATH CLASS

FRIDAY 13

Dear Dumb Diary,

I got the first **"BAND"** applications today. I'm **not** telling these people that they're applying for the position of *Fourth Friend*, because I don't want any of them to be too disappointed when they don't get the job. Pretty friendly of me, right?

I spoke with the following three applicants at lunch. They were all breezy and chummy, but I felt like I should keep the atmosphere more official. After all, I'm selecting what will probably be a lifelong friend here, so I need to ask a few important questions.

Professional expression

Professional posture

Professional clipboard (the most official thing you can write on)

ARTIST'S RENDERING OF APPLICANT

Applicant's name: Margaret

First Impression: Margaret is nice, but not that interesting. She is like a half slice of toast with a small amount of diet jelly on it.

Known Weirdnesses: Margaret is a pencil chewer and is, therefore, beaverish.

"Why do you think you'd be right for this position?" Margaret removed the pencil from her mouth long enough to respond: "You know what — forget it. I don't want to be in your band."

Interviewer notes: I'm a bit concerned that pencils are a gateway chew toy that could lead to more dangerous chew toys like the fingers of bandmates. For this reason, as well as the beaverishness, this application is: REJECTED.

Artist's rendering of Applicant

Applicant's name: Elizabeth

First Impression: Elizabeth is politely not pretty — even less pretty than Isabella — which I find friendly.

Known Weirdnesses: Spittish. Once I saw Elizabeth sneeze in front of a window, and the spit mist was so extreme that I saw a rainbow in her spew cloud.

"Why do you think you'd be right for this position?" Elizabeth responded, "I'd like to hang around with Angeline. She's in the band, too, right?"

Interviewer notes: Of all the ways to have the name Elizabeth (Beth, Betsy, Liz, Lizbeth, Lizzy, Betty, Eliza) she has chosen the least cute one, and that troubles me. I give her points for her willingness to be the ugliest girl in the group, but I don't want to get all spitted on, plus she seems to have an unhealthy obsession about Angeline so this one is also: REJECTED.

Artist's rendering of Applicant

similar to life-size

Applicant's name: Shannon

First Impression: Shannon is small and would be easy to carry if a Shannon-carrying situation were to arise.

Known Weirdnesses: Shannon once swallowed a pretzel incorrectly at a water park and has tragically lost the ability to burp.

"Why do you think you'd be right for this position?" Shannon's response: "I'm really reliable and small, which makes me easy to carry."

Interviewer notes: Shannon keeps herself very clean, and I really can't stress how much I admire the fact that she is small. But I'm worried that the digestive system of a person incapable of discharging gas through her mouth might have to compensate in other ways, and for that reason I must mark this application: REJECTED.

Wow. Three whole applications, and not **one** lifelong friend in the bunch. Making new friends is hard. How can you tell which ones will always be there for you, doing what you tell them, and giving you junk?

I think maybe tomorrow I'm going to have to really take a look at what friendship means. Maybe if I dig down deep and meditate on it, TV will give me the answer.

Saturday 14

Dear Dumb Diary,

Okay, brace yourself. **TV may not be an expert on everything.** This came as quite a blow to me, because TV always seems so confident. On the subject of friendship, for instance, there are a lot of issues.

1.   On television, friends often get mad at each other and then are friends again within 22 minutes or so. In the real world, it generally takes about that long just to figure out how you're going to **get even** with somebody.

2.   *TV-mad* isn't like *real-world-mad*. On TV, people throw pies at each other when they get angry. If Isabella gets mad, she's not going to throw a pie. She's going to throw the baker at you.

3.   On TV, groups of people are friends for a **reason**. Like, there's a smart one, and a pretty one, and a sporty one, and a scary one. Are we supposed to be choosing our friends based on some reason? I hope not. I spent more time picking out my socks this morning than I did picking out Isabella.

Even when the group of friends is made up of animal characters, they're all different. It's like, one is a lion, one is an ostrich, one is a zebra, and one is an antelope. In the wild, a group like this wouldn't be thought of as a group of friends. This would be thought of as a lion and his talking lunch.

My conclusion is this: TV is a very simpleminded device. It specializes largely in cola commercials and people throwing balls. Evidently, it just can't explain the **truly mystifying** things in the world, like why Grandpa wears his pants up under his armpits, or how friendships work.

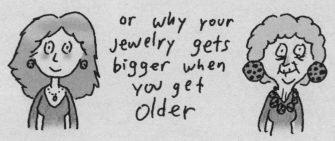

or why your jewelry gets bigger when you get older

Sunday 15

Dear Dumb Diary,

This morning, I called Isabella to come over and pretend to do homework, as we often do on Sundays, but she wasn't home. I guess I could have called my Automatic Friend Angeline to see if she wanted to come over, but I wasn't feeling **THAT** automatic.

It worked out okay, anyway. I made today an Art Day. I started my final piece for the Art Show today, and I think it may turn out to be **the greatest art that has ever been made by a human girl.**

I'm going to use sequins, rhinestones, and glitter, which is pretty much the first thing an artist needs when they are going to commit art.

They ALSO HAVe to start acting in an arty wAY. This is called AN ARTITUDE.

I began my relationship with glitter pretty early in life. Although, back then, I was using cereal for glitter and slobber for glue. And for paper I used my face. And it was accidental. But all of the same principles apply.

(Note to future Jamie: If your baby is all sticky and grimy, just roll him in glitter. It will stick like glue and your baby will instantly be the envy of all the other moms with unsparkly children.)

feel the glamour!

In second grade, I tried to teach Isabella how to do glitter and she couldn't quite understand the concept of wanting to make something prettier. I remember she kept asking things like, "Will dis make it more explodey?"

In third grade, she taught me how to buy things and make it look like your mean older brothers did it. She just kept track of the things her brothers asked her mom for. If her mom said no, Isabella would order those things online. That made it **look** like her brothers had done it, and it would get them grounded for months and months. **So cute!**

I wish she had come over today.

Dear Dumb Diary,

So in math today, **guess who actually answered a question correctly**. That's right: ISABELLA. Nothing written on her hand, no Jamie whispering to her. She Just Answered.

Now, normally I would assume that it was a lucky guess. Or it was a typical ISABELLA-ANSWER, like when in social studies they asked her how many pharaohs had been mummified in ancient Egypt and Isabella answered, "All of 'em."

But math doesn't work well with guesses or Isabella-answers. So how did Isabella pull this off? It was a real puzzle until I noticed, dangling from between the pages of her math book like a guilty bookmark, a two-foot-long blond hair.

It was obvious. Angeline and Isabella studied together. **ON SUNDAY.** A day, which I think most people would admit, is **MY PRIVATE PROPERTY** for studying on with Isabella. Pretending to study on Sunday is a tradition that goes back with Isabella and me for **AN ENTIRE GENERATION,** so far.

A CENTURY FROM NOW, THIS WILL BE A

HUNDRED-YEAR-OLD TRADITION!

S.B.Fs

(SHRIVELED BEST FRIENDS)

I brought it up casually at Isabella's locker.

"Nice job on the math today," I said, laying a **clever trap** for her.

"Angeline came over to my house yesterday and helped me study," she said, not giving me cause to cleverly trap her any further.

"I called you to come over and study. But there was no answer," I said.

Isabella said nothing. She blinked a couple times, and breathed, but she didn't apologize — and this would have been the perfect time. I know that if she fails math she'll have to take summer school, and when she comes over to study at my house we never get anything done. Still. If she won't apologize for studying with Angeline, maybe she should at least apologize for being **dumb at math**.

I'm just saying that I think somebody owes me an apology. Maybe several people do. Maybe the Universe does.

A muffin Basket and Balloon would be nice, too.

This new scandal makes it clear that I'm getting edged out of this three-way friendship even faster than I thought. But I can't go all mental about it. It's not like I *own* Isabella.

Or do I?

I do call her **MY** friend, the same way I call them **MY** socks or **MY** infection. Nobody would ever suggest that the infection belongs to itself.

So maybe I do kind of own her.

I just have to speed up the Friend Application process, that's all there is to it. I have to acquire that fourth friend to distract Angeline so I can have my best friend back. I'm not going to let my **BFF** turn into a **BFIL**. (That's Best Friend I Lost.) No, instead, I'm going to stay up late and make some more **"JOIN OUR BAND"** flyers.

Fasten your seat belts. It's going to be a glittery night.

And lo, the Talent shall fall like Rain.

JAMIE, ISABELLA
AND ANGELINE
INVITE YOU TO BE THE
4th MEMBER OF OUR
BAND AND PERFORM
WITH US IN THE
TALENT SHOW!
APPLICANTS MUST BE NICE AND FRIENDLY BUT NOT SO FRIENDLY THAT YOU'RE ALWAYS TRYING TO STEAL OTHER PEOPLE'S FRIENDS.
SEE JAMIE IN THE LUNCHROOM TO APPLY.
thank you for not being male.

Tuesday 17

Dear Dumb Diary,

**NOW THAT'S WHAT I'M TALKIN'
ABOUT.** I put up the new, better, sparklier flyers
and I got a better quality of applicant today. Sure,
I was blowing glitter out of my nose all morning, but
with one notable exception, it was worth it. I think
I just might be able to pull the right person out of
this **friend herd.**

I know that it's wrong to exclude boys, but
Hudson would have auditioned and then we'd have
the duh-rama of him rediscovering his feelings
for me, and that would drive another wedge
between me and Isabella, and I really can't let that
happen.

Let's review, shall we?

HORNK

BLOWING GLITTER
COULD BE BEAUTIFUL
IF IT WASN'T SO GROSS

Artist's rendering of Applicant

Applicant's name: Anika

First Impression: Anika is good at fashion things and prettiness. These qualities could make her the perfect toy to distract Angeline with.

Known Weirdnesses: Anika has no known weirdnesses. This concerns me because, as is the case with **all** non-weird people, whatever her weirdnesses are, they are SO weird that she must be working very hard to keep them hidden.

"Why do you think you'd be right for this position?" Anika's response: "I'm a good singer."

Interviewer notes: Even though she didn't sing her response, I'm willing to believe that Anika is a good singer, although I suspect that most truly good singers sing everything they say. She may not be BFF material, but she could be a BFFN (Best Friend For Now). I'm going to mark this application: REJECTED.

Applicant's name: Fléurrål Mjångîi-Shmørp. Or something like that.

First Impression: Fléurrål is foreign, and therefore exotic. She hasn't been in our country long, so she is still interesting.

Known Weirdnesses: One never really knows, when evaluating someone from far away, what aspects of their behavior are simply new to you and what parts are as crazy as an outhouse rat. Fléurrål, for example, always smells like some kind of turnip herb soup and wears her hair in braids that look like the climbing rope in the gym.

Also, Foreigners seem to enjoy

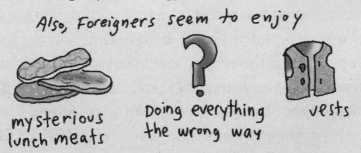

mysterious lunch meats

Doing everything the wrong way

vests

"Why do you think you'd be right for this position?" Fléurrål's response: "Yes. I can write in this position." And then to prove it, she pulled out a notebook and wrote in that position. She wrote this: HAV A NICE DAY JØMIÉ.
Interviewer notes: I can teach her that my name is Jamie, not Jømié, so that's not a huge problem. Isabella is naturally suspicious of anybody from another country, so Fléurrål would be all Angeline's responsibility. I'm going to mark this application: MAYBE.

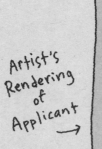

Artist's Rendering of Applicant →

Applicant's name: My Aunt Carol, who shouldn't be auditioning.

First Impression: Aunt Carol works here at the school and only came down to apply because she saw the flyers. I'm sure she thought she was being cute.

Known Weirdnesses: Aunt Carol, being my aunt and married, is old — which is one of the weirdest things a person can choose to be.

"Why do you think you'd be right for this position?" Aunt Carol's response: (The interviewer must point out that Aunt Carol tried to imitate dumb-girl speech and pretended to chew gum as she responded, which I think was probably meant as an insult to everybody my age.) "Well, I've known you since you were a baby and I'm super-fun and I still like you even though you got me kicked out of a movie for the first time in my life and I'll

look great dancing up onstage with you guys. Want to see?"

Interviewer notes: At this point, the applicant stood up and would have danced in front of everybody except for the fact that I stopped her and saved myself from extreme embarrassment, and saved the world from being sickened by Aunt Dancing. This, plus the fact that Aunt Carol can't be in the student Talent Show due to the fact she is **NOT A STUDENT,** requires that I mark her application: **REJECTED.**

Angeline and Isabella wandered over to the auditions at the end of lunch to find out how things were going. I told them that we'd had a few promising auditions today, and that I thought we'd have that fourth band member soon.

Hudson was circling like a shark, watching us talk and transmitting crush vibrations in Isabella's direction. That's *Isabella's* direction, and not Angeline's. I have to keep reminding myself.

I saw Angeline notice Hudson and I think I might have detected something. Was it a tinge of disappointment?

It seems like Angeline's one ability, which is to be **unreasonably pretty,** is no longer working against Hudson. I guess maybe she just doesn't have it anymore.

GOSH isn't it just soooo SAD when the BEAUTIFUL AND PERFECT DON'T GET THEIR WAY? OH. BOO. HOO.

Wednesday 18

Dear Dumb Diary,

In art today, Miss Anderson wanted to talk about all of our portraits from last week — what was successful about them, and how they could be better. The picture of me that T.U.K.W.N.I.F. drew didn't get the big laugh it got last time. It looked like maybe he went back and spent a little more time on it.

Don't get me wrong, he still can't draw, but at least the portrait looked a lot less like a chimpanzee and a clown had a baby and then tied a mop to its head and used it to clean out a stable.

My drawing of T.U.K. was really good. I'm not being conceited — sometimes if you do something well, you just have to confess that you did. I'm good at this. I'm not the best in the world, but I rock. In the future, I could rock seriously, big-time, and **out loud.**

YEAH. I ROCK.

me too.

The portrait Angeline did of Isabella was just clumsy and awkward, and not at all up to the high standards I have set for drawing Isabella these many years.

But most troubling was the drawing Isabella did of Angeline.

It was actually *kind of good*.

When Isabella draws me, she doesn't really spend any time on it. It's never more than a smiley face with hair.

But Angeline had a whole body and hair and eyelashes and all that stuff. Isabella really spent a lot of time on the drawing, like she cared how it looked, even though Isabella doesn't really care how anything looks. Often, her Halloween costumes consist of a piece of paper taped to her shirt, stating what she's supposed to be.

I really, **really** wanted to talk to Isabella about this, and maybe even bawl her out and then run, because that's the best and smartest thing to do after you bawl her out.

But how do you even say something like that without sounding like a lunatic? "Isabella, I demand that you be my friend much more than you are Angeline's friend. In doing so, you should always draw me better than you draw Angeline. Always. And also, I demand that we both forget the fact that the Universe made Angeline an Automatic Friend and we go back to when I was on her case all the time."

But I can't say any of that.

All I can say is: Thanks a lot, Isabella. Thanks for being such a good friend.

Of course I can't *really* say that, I can only write it. But I'm writing it **totally sarcastically** and **rather meanly.**

I'm just going to work on my masterpiece more.

The Human face is not big enough for the scowls it must sometimes scowl.

Thursday 19

Dear Dumb Diary,

More people auditioned for friend/bandmate today at lunch. Wait until you get a load of this.

I was hoping for some truly interesting applicants....

Artist's rendering of Applicant

Applicant's name: Emmily (She spells it with two *m*'s because she says it reminds her of candy that way.)

First Impression: Emmily is nice, and easily the dumbest girl in my grade — maybe in any grade. But I've found that the witless are often quite charming, and a lot of fun to have around as they are easy to trick, although they are often spilly.

Known Weirdnesses: I've seen her reflection startle her when she walks past a mirror.

"Why do you think you'd be right for this position?" Emmily's response: "I'm really smart and good with numbers. Are you going to finish those chips? Also, I'm smart."

Interviewer's comments: Would Emmily make a good friend? I don't know. She finished my chips before I could answer the question, so in that way she reminds me of Isabella. As predicted in my first impression, she did spill her milk during the interview. Four times.

I suppose I should mark this application: MAYBE.

Artist's rendering of applicant

Applicant's name: Nadia

First Impression: Nadia is a little vampirey.

Known Weirdnesses: Nadia only dresses in black and wears black fingernail polish and her lunch consisted entirely of black food. I have to give her extra points for this, because I don't even know where you could find a black lunch.

"Why do you think you'd be right for this position?" Nadia's response: "I want to introduce a new kind of music to the world that is based mostly on the sounds you make when you stub your toe."

Interviewer's comments: Would Nadia make a good friend? I don't know. She likes to gross people out, and she scratched me.

I guess I'll mark this application: PROBABLY.

Artist's rendering of Applicant

Applicant's name: T.U.K.W.N.I.F.
First Impression: Skip this.
Known Weirdnesses: Skip this.
"Why do you think you'd be right for this position?" Skip this, too.
Interviewer's comments: I explained that the audition wasn't open to dudes. T.U.K. apologized, but before he did, I saw his face turn from just ugly to ugly-sad. He walked away slowly, and I think I learned something: In a way, ugly-sad isn't purely ugly — it's also kind of funny-looking.

Needless to say, I'm marking this application: **DOUBLE SUPER REJECTED.**

UGLY

UGLIEREST

And now I'm just lost.

I've reviewed the applications over and over and I can't figure it out. I marked scratchy vampire girl as a **PROBABLY**? And I rejected Anika, who I've known for a long time and really like? I'm beginning to think I don't even know what makes people friends.

And if that's the case, there's only one thing we can be absolutely sure of: Nobody else knows, either.

Other Things Nobody Knows...

why the HAIR in your nose doesn't grow as long as the hair on your head.

why DAD always buys DUMB SHOES when the good ones are right NEXT TO THEM.

wait. in grandpa's case it sort of does.

Friday 20

Dear Dumb Diary,

Today at school, Isabella and Angeline wanted to know who our fourth band member was, so I had to choose somebody. I didn't know what to say.

"Elizabeth," I said finally.

"Fine." Isabella shrugged.

"She's **spitty**, you know."

"I've been spat on," Isabella said, chuckling a little. I knew it was true. Her brothers often opened her door at bedtime to give her a good-night spritz.

"Or maybe Anika," I said. "Or Nadia the vampire."

"Anika's fine," Isabella said. "Or Nadia. Whatever."

Angeline just sat there and smiled. I don't think either one of them even cared who I picked.

NOT even caring

Of course they didn't care. They didn't understand that I was choosing our new BFF. They still thought this was only about picking a bandmate for the Talent Show.

"Shannon," I said. I couldn't make up my mind. Choosing a lifelong friend is a lot of pressure. "It's Shannon."

"Okay!" Isabella barked. "It's Shannon then, right? Shannon? We're all in agreement here? Shannon? Our new band member is Shannon?"

I nodded. Angeline nodded.

Later on, I called Emmily to tell her she made the band.

When she Hears a ring, Emmily might answer....

HELLO?

HELLO?

HELLO?

A carrot

The Cat

The phone

We Must Be patient when phoning the Stupid.

Saturday 21

Dear Dumb Diary,

Today was our first rehearsal. My dad let us use the garage because, as he explained to my mom, he didn't want to stand in the way of talent. Although, I remember that he was also supposed to clean out the garage this weekend, and now our talent was giving him an afternoon on the couch.

Isabella just shook her head when Emmily showed up to rehearsal. Angeline was overjoyed, but Angeline spends a lot of time overjoyed, so for her, it was probably just **regular old joyed.**

Angeline Regular Old Joyed

Angeline OVERJOYED (NOTE smile actually rips free from face)

We finally found a song we all knew the lyrics to, and we practiced lip-synching. The song we chose has a lot of *s*'s in it, so it's a good thing I didn't go with Elizabeth as our fourth member, or the whole front row would have been lathered up in her **mouth-suds**.

After practicing for a while, we talked about how we're going to get instruments to pretend to play. Angeline said she was sure she could get us what we needed. She said the music teacher was always happy to encourage music. Even fake music.

Angeline and Emmily talked a lot, so Isabella and I goofed around more than we had in a while. It felt like old times. Yes indeed, Emmily is just what this three-way friendship needed — a Fourth Friend to divide the friendship into two smaller friendships.

I can't wait to see how much we improve tomorrow.

It was so much fun hanging with Isabella that I wanted to send her a card...

I treasure how the same people and things make us both want to barf.

But you can never seem to find one that says how you feel.

Sunday 22

Dear Dumb Diary,

    Isabella and Angeline brought their puppies, Bubblegum Duchess and Prince Fuzzybutt, to visit their **sisterpuppy**, Stinkette. They all played with their **dogdad**, Stinker, in the backyard while we created fake musical genius in the garage.

    I'm beginning to think that professional bands must practice fairly often, because after three **FULL** hours of pretending to sing today, I'm not sure we got any better.

Really, it was only an hour of practice. We spent the rest of the time on the extremely important tasks of choosing a band name and discussing wardrobe.

We narrowed the band names down to these, and we'll vote on them later:

The Jamie Kelly Experience
Friends R 4
Awesomeness Unleashed
The Brother Sisters (Okay, this was *all* Emmily's idea. She said that since brother bands are really popular, that this would be a good name.)

my fake playing is pretty much as good as real playing.

Wardrobe wasn't an issue for Angeline, of course, since she would look good in a sweater knitted from living earthworms. But for those of us with human DNA, wardrobe IS an issue.

We finally decided on jeans, black T-shirts, and sunglasses, because they're the only things we all own one of. For some reason, Emmily has enough clown outfits to go around, and she offered to let us borrow them. But clowns are kind of a problem for me since I happen to know that they are the evil living dead that are using beepy noses and balloon animals to fool us.

I'm just not a fan of the Living DeaD.

Angeline found a couple guitars somewhere, so I thought we looked pretty authentic as we faked it, although I'm sure I saw some frustration in Isabella's eyes.

ONLY A **TRUE** BFF CAN READ YOUR EYES

HOSTILITY

ENVY

CONCERN

SMELLS SOMETHING

FRUSTRATION

REVENGEY

Monday 23

Dear Dumb Diary,

I was supposed to have read a chapter in my "classic" book by now, but I haven't gotten around to it. Most of my free time has been devoted to my masterpiece for the Art Show and fake singing in the mirror. If everyone votes to call the band The Jamie Kelly Experience, a lot of eyes will be fixed on my performance in particular. I owe it to the fans to fake it well.

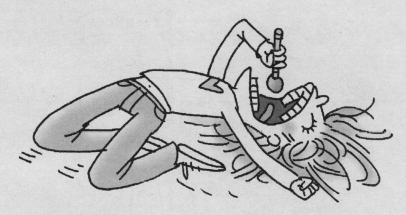

One of my ROCKiNeST SiNGiNG poses — I call this THE DYING HOWLER MONKEY.

I saw Hudson talking to Angeline by her locker today, which normally would have **normal-bothered** me, but this time it bothered me **a lot** because Hudson currently has a crush-in-progress on Isabella. Even though Isabella couldn't care less, he is still technically her crush-property until she officially says otherwise. This rule is particularly important among **FRIENDS**. Since Angeline is now one of those, automatically, it's inexcusable for her to violate this rule.

After Hudson walked away, I gave her a severe talking to, kind of.

"So," I said, implying a lot more than that, "what's up with Hudson?"

Angeline shrugged. "He wanted to know how our band was coming along."

"Was he asking about Isabella or you?" I asked with fake nonchalance.

"He was asking about all of us. You, me, Emmily, and Isabella. Mostly Isabella."

For a moment, I had forgotten that Emmily existed, which makes me wonder if she's trying hard enough to be my friend.

"Right. Emmily," I covered perfectly. "What did you tell him?"

Angeline pulled out a brush and slipped it through her hair. I had never noticed before, but her hair makes a kind of lovely, floaty **harp sound** when she brushes it. She must have forgotten that, or she surely would have used the technique on Hudson.

"I told him I think our performance is going to be pretty funny."

I narrowed my eyes. "Did you mean like HA-HA funny, or MELT-INTO-A-STEAMING-PILE-OF-EMBARRASSING-SHAME funny?"

Angeline closed her locker and looked at me with an expression far more serious than is usually seen on her perky face: "Funny, Jamie. I guess it will just be funny."

As she walked away, I realized that it bothered me somehow to see Angeline less than her usual perky ball of pure perk. I guess her inability to be **Lovely-on-Demand** is really bugging her.

First Aid you probably do when somebody Loses their Perky

1. perform mouth-to-mouth resuscitation, but do it with Butterfly-kisses on their cheek.

2. Inject them with some kind of pretty, rainbow-colored medicine.

3. put their arm in a cast with a kitten inside for PERMANENT PETTING.

Tuesday 24

Dear Dumb Diary,

 The Art Show is coming up, so I really have to dig in and finish my project. I don't have much time to write tonight, because I'll be up late practicing extreme **glitterization**.
 But I did have a profound thought on friendship that I needed to record: What if I met a really great person who would be a really great friend, but their name rhymed with mine? Like Mamie or Damie. (I've never heard of those names, but people can name their babies anything, like Football, or Napoleon, or Angeline.) It would be hard to be friends with our dumb rhyming names ("Here come Jamie and Mamie!"), so how would we ever decide who would have to change her name? And after we decided, what would she change her name to?

SOME NAMES IT WOULD BE OKAY FOR MY FRIENDS TO HAVE
1. SUSANNN   3. HAMSTERIA
2. MOLAR   4. MAYBE NOT MOLAR

Wednesday 25

Dear Dumb Diary,

I took my art project in to school today. I was up way later than I was supposed to be last night, and I created something that could only be called *magnificent*.

Actually, it could also be called *spectacular*. And *fabulous*. I guess it could be called lots of things. But now there's one thing it won't be called: **a Prize Winner**.

Miss Anderson dropped the bomb on us in today's art class: They canceled the Art Show. There's only so much money in the school budget this year, so lots of things are getting canceled.

Miss Anderson said that more kids participate in the Talent Show, so it only seemed fair to choose that over the Art Show. If the budget improves, maybe they'll do both next year.

It just seems so unfair that things have to be fair all the time.

Fairness is the most unfair thing in the world.

Thursday 26

Dear Dumb Diary,

I was so depressed about the Art Show being canceled that **I ate the meat loaf today.** I didn't care. I ate a whole serving. Isabella watched me. I was getting ready to eat a second helping, but Miss Bruntford stopped me.

"You really shouldn't eat too much — 'meat,' let's call it — in one sitting," she said.

Full of meat loaf and glumness, I told Isabella that I'm dropping out of the Talent Show. I don't want to drop out. More than anything, I'd like to go on with Isabella and all, but in this mood, I'd blow the whole thing for them. I told her that she should go on with Angeline and do her magic act, and really fool the idiots in the audience.

Isabella was *not* happy. "You're just going to walk out on me?" she said. "The show is tomorrow."

I *did* kind of walk out on her, and I wanted to take it back, but it was for all the right reasons. The Talent Show was really important to me, but I know I couldn't act all happy participating in a show that the school had decided to do instead of the Art Show. I guess I'm not that good at acting, after all.

I'm probably no longer qualified to pronounce it as *"duh-rama."*

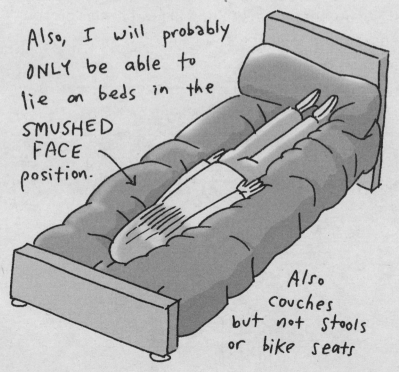

Also, I will probably ONLY be able to lie on beds in the SMUSHED FACE position.

Also couches but not stools or bike seats

Isabella stared at me in such an angry way that it made me think about how happy I was that there were witnesses around. Then she quietly said that she understood, and drank my milk without asking. I could tell that she was pretending that it was all of my precious bodily fluids.

I watched her walk out of the lunchroom. She stopped just long enough to talk to Angeline. I couldn't tell what they were saying, but Angeline shot a furious look my way, and I swear I saw her eyes turn from baby-blue to baby-red.

As hard as it is to find BFFs, it seems pretty easy to lose them.

After school, I just sat on my bed for a long time and watched Stinkette chew up Stinker's beloved Grossnasty. I still don't understand why he doesn't go all crazy werewolf on her for it. Maybe he's just too dumb to notice.

Stinkette Teaches Us How To Enjoy The Disgusting Chew Toy.

Approach carefully. Maybe has come to Life!

Pounce hardfully! Is clever dangerous prey.

Chew Chewfully for 6 minutes. Is delicious.

Nap. Hunting and killing is exhausting.

Repeat entire process.

Friday 27

Dear Dumb Diary,

The Talent Show was tonight. I've been mad all day about the Art Show, but my parents made me go to the Talent Show — and I'm glad they did.

It was long, and pretty boring at times. There was the usual assortment of acts: a baton twirler, a violin player, and a kid who tried to juggle (but I'm pretty sure he just started practicing this morning).

Isabella did her magic act — but not with Angeline. She had Emmily assisting her. But here's the thing. You know how Isabella's main interest in magic is fooling people? She had never in her wildest dreams hoped to find a magician's assistant who would be *easier to fool than the audience*.

Emmily was shocked and amazed by everything Isabella did. She gasped and clapped at each little trick. And her astonishment was contagious.

the clapping of PURE AMAZEMENT

Isabella just went with it. Toward the end, Isabella started laughing a little, and the audience laughed and Emmily laughed and it was hard to tell who was laughing at what. I've seen Isabella do these magic tricks a million times, and I've never enjoyed them more than when I watched Emmily — sweet, stupid Emmily — get completely taken in by Isabella's wizardry. I could tell that Isabella had never enjoyed them more, either.

A note to magicians everywhere: **Get Yourself an Emmily.**

The next act was — believe it or not —
T.U.K.W.N.I.F. They rolled out a piano for him to
play, but he turned it so we couldn't see him, just
the front of the piano, which I thought was a pretty
reasonable way to hide his face from the audience.
But I was wrong — he turned it like that because
there was something on the front of the piano.

My Art Show drawing. For a second, I didn't
really recognize it. When you see something that's
totally unexpected, your brain can't understand
what you're seeing: like if you found your shoes
in the refrigerator or saw your custodian walking
down the street in a dress. (To be fair, that might
not have been him.)

But, there it was, and for his entire song, it
glittered and shimmered and sparkled in the bright
spotlight even more beautifully and dazzlingly than
I knew it could. T.U.K. made the school look at my
drawing for a full four minutes, and he did a pretty
good job on the piano. Who knew he could play?

He stood up and took a bow, and for a
second, I think I very nearly remembered his name.

POWERFUL RAYS
OF UTTER BEAUTY
RADIATING from my
ART

Next, Nadia, Anika, Margaret, and Fléurrål came out and lip-synched a song. As embarrassingly horrible and awful as they were, they were at least twice as good as we would have been.

At that moment, I realized how fortunate we were that **The Jamie Kelly Experience** did not perform.

Finally, Angeline came out with a *guitar*.

OMG. She was going to do our lip-synching act **ALL BY HERSELF.**

I felt a wave of sickness come over me. Part of me knew it would be delicious to watch Angeline fry in the spotlight's scorching flames of embarrassment. (You can't even put aloe on those kinds of burns.) But part of me weirdly wanted to protect her from it, because this was pretty much my fault.

I started to stand up. I don't know what I was planning to do. I suppose I was going to scream, **"Stop!"** and pull her off the stage or maybe throw a shoe at the lighting guy, but I didn't have to do either one.

Because Angeline **didn't** start the lip-synching act. She just stood there and talked.

"The funding for the Art Show was cut," she said, "and we need your help so it can go on next month as planned. Please drop a dollar or whatever you can in the donation buckets by the exit as you leave tonight. Thank you."

And maybe that would have raised a buck or two, but she wasn't done. Because then Angeline turned on those switches inside that she had kept turned off all month. It was like watching some immense nuclear power plant activate and then slowly begin generating electricity.

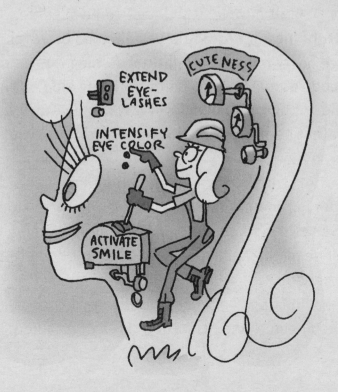

First, the **smile**; the spotlight hit Angeline's gleaming white teeth and a blinding ray of toothy beauty blazed into the audience. Then she batted her long **eyelashes**. They created a breeze that we all felt flutter across our faces. And when she was up to full output, she tossed her **glimmering hair** back and forth in slow motion, causing every hand in the auditorium to plunge helplessly into pockets and purses and fork over what added up to more than three hundred bucks — much more than they needed to put on the Art Show.

Angeline did that for me. I didn't ask for it. I didn't expect it. Angeline hadn't *lost* her gorgeousness — she could turn on the charm anytime she wanted. She had been *intentionally* not using it on Hudson. And now I'm sure it was for Isabella's sake.

You could actually smell her delicious eyelash aroma.

Right after the show, I caught up to Angeline and Isabella in the hall.

"You're not mad?" I said.

"We **were** mad," Isabella said. "For a minute." And then shoved me hard into the wall to show me that she wasn't mad anymore. I shoved her back to show how happy I was that I hadn't lost my BFF.

Aunt Carol and Uncle Dan walked over to say hi.

"Nice job, everybody," he said. "And good news about the Art Show. Thanks to the donations, that's back on."

And then he asked Angeline why she hadn't played her guitar.

"Changed my mind," she said.

"You can *play* that?" I blurted out.

Uncle Dan laughed. "She's been taking lessons for years. She's amazing. She would have won the Talent Show hands down — no offense, Isabella. But you guys have a band or something, don't you? You knew she could play."

And then it happened. Before I could stop myself, I actually **GAVE ANGELINE A HEARTFELT HUG** and I even thanked her. It was a really quiet whispered "thank you," but I'm pretty sure she heard it because she whispered back an equally quiet "You're welcome" that I very nearly heard.

It was so weird. I never hug Isabella, and we've been BFFs forever. But it didn't seem right to shove Angeline.

Angeline hugged me back. Really hard. Like a crazy person.

Am I friends with Angeline? Can I be friends with somebody that is so perfect all the time? Can I overcome Angeline's perfection handicap?

Dear Dumb Diary,

This morning while I was watching TV (and by the way, I've lost some respect for its expertness), the doorbell rang. My mom answered the door.

"Jamie — it's for you. Somebody named Tuc or Tuckster or something like that. The boy who played the piano last night."

I couldn't believe it. **He actually goes by T.U.K.W.N.I.F.?!**

When I went to the door, he had my drawing.

"I wanted to get this back to you right away. I knew you'd want it," he said.

"Thanks. And thanks for making it part of your act. That was really great," I said, and he smiled. It was weird, because when he smiled, like, at least a gallon of ugly poured off his face.

"It was Isabella's idea. But I agreed with her right away. She didn't have to threaten me like that."

I knew just what he was talking about. "Sometimes she does that without thinking. A threat is just like 'please' to her," I said.

T.U.K.W.N.I.F. nodded. "I'm glad the Art Show is going on after all. You're really going to want to hang this one up."

He was right. I did want to hang it up. It's probably the best drawing I've ever done.

But standing there looking at him, something changed my mind. "I was thinking of putting that other one up," I said. "The portrait I did of you. If that's okay."

Then T.U.K.W.N.I.F.'s face did all sorts of things. It was confused, then happy, then confused again, then really happy. He nodded and laughed, and even more ugly poured off his face.

"But I want to make sure I spell your name right," I cleverly said. I still couldn't remember it, and this was an ingenious way to get it.

"T-U-," he began, "C-K-E-R."

"Tucker? *Your name is Tucker?* Really?" I laughed. "That's easy to remember."

He looked a little confused, but I decided not to explain.

I watched him walk down the sidewalk. A few of his friends had been waiting for him. All of a sudden, I almost couldn't remember why I've called him T.U.K.W.N.I.F. all these years.

He changed like the opposite of a werewolf

Later today, Isabella popped in unannounced, which is her favorite way to pop. She said she wanted to come over today because tomorrow she'd be studying with Angeline, and we need at least one day each weekend to just hang. She missed our fake homework Sundays, too. I thanked her for threatening Tucker for me, and she cutely blushed.

She said that she thinks, with Angeline's help, she won't have to go to summer school and watch me and Angeline having fun out the window without her. That mattered to Isabella. Turns out, Isabella is a little possessive, too.

But not about Hudson. Earlier this morning, I had called Isabella and begged her to tell Angeline that she was officially throwing him away. That way, if Angeline wanted to work her voodoo on him, it was okay with Isabella. Hudson was the first boy to ever have a crush on Isabella, so it was very difficult for her to just give him away like that. Isabella doesn't even like throwing old shoes away.

"You were right, Jamie. Angeline *is* protecting me from summer school. And she got your Art Show back for you, even though you bailed on us. I called her and told her that I didn't care about Hudson, and it made her really happy." It was such a kind thing for Isabella to do that I couldn't breathe for a second because I thought that maybe she was dying.

Isabella smiled. "And did you see how Angeline worked the bucks from the crowd? It's like I've said all along, being friends with her is a good idea. She's going to be a **very** handy friend to have."

So now it comes out: Isabella thinks we *own* Angeline, like our socks, or our infections.

And we've been thinking of Hudson the exact same way.

Isabella must think of me that way, and Angeline probably does, too.

Is this how friendships work? Maybe we really **are** just like each other's socks or infections.

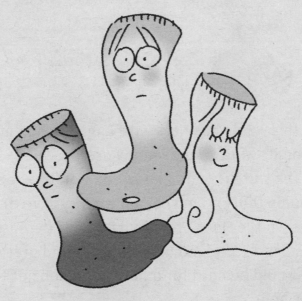

Isabella and I made plans to meet tomorrow at Angeline's house after they do their math stuff. We called Emmily to meet us, too, even though it took us twenty minutes to give her directions.

Emmily lives **four doors down** from Angeline.

If Emmily could see out her Belly Button, she might not ever use her head.

BYE!

BRING BACK GUM

This whole business with Angeline had me questioning what friends really are.

The truth is (and I know you won't believe this, Dumb Diary), I may be an **eensy, weensy, beensy** bit jealous of Angeline. In my defense, she is so perfectly kind and pleasant and pretty that it would be hard for a normal person not to despise her.

I thought that since we were kind of related by the marriage of our aunt and uncle AND by the puppies that our dogs had together, that we were some sort of cousins or something and that made us Automatic Friends. But just being relatives really doesn't make you *automatically* friends.

I mean, I think of Aunt Carol as a friend, and I think of my parents as friends when they're not telling me what to do or making me eat Mom's cooking. Stinker thinks of his dogdaughter, Stinkette, as a friend. But some relatives aren't really friends, like Isabella's brothers, who are archenemies she eats dinner with every night.

And now I think there is no such thing as an *Automatic* Friend.

PRETTY EYES
PLUS
PRETTY HAIR
PLUS
PRETTY SMILE
EQUALS
PRETTY ANNOYING

OK sometimes MATH Does MAKE SENSE.

I used to think that friends were there to give you things or to do things for you. They will, of course, but actually, that's what friends **aren't** for.

It's just the **opposite**.

If you want to know who your friends are, look at the people you do things *for*, or who you give things *to* — whether it's saving them from a shark, or giving them a heartfelt crazy-person hug, or letting them have Hudson Rivers. Or maybe you're saving an Art Show for them, doing a drawing of them, or going along with their dumb band idea even though you know your magic act would be way better. Or maybe you're letting them have your Grossnasty.

Especially letting them have your Grossnasty.

There's no way around this: Angeline is my friend. And I just can't stand it.

Thanks for listening, Dumb Diary,

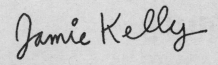

P.S. I asked Isabella about the drawing she did of Angeline, and why it had so much great detail, and why the drawings she did of me were always so simple.

"Because," she said, "I always wanted to finish mine as fast as possible so I could watch you draw. Angeline watches you draw, too — she's so jealous. "

Angeline, jealous of me? It was such a sweet thing to say that I punched her in the arm for it, **hard**. And Isabella warmly punched me back.

#1: Let's Pretend This
Never Happened

#2: My Pants Are
Haunted!

#3: Am I the Princess or
the Frog?

#4: Never Do
Anything, Ever

#5: Can Adults Become
Human?

#6: The Problem With Here
Is That It's Where I'm From

#7: Never Underestimate
Your Dumbness

#8: It's Not My Fault I
Know Everything

#9: That's What Friends
<u>Aren't</u> For

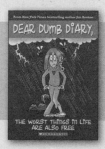

#10: The Worst Things In
Life Are Also Free

#11: Okay, So Maybe I Do
Have Superpowers

#12: Me! (Just Like You,
Only Better)

Money can't buy happiness.
But it can buy an awesome summer vacation.

Dear Dumb Diary,

Isabella asked her mom for money, but since Isabella's mom has THREE children, she is three times meaner than a mom with only one, and said no. We tried to escape the room as soon as we saw her mouth begin to form ADULT WISDOM, but she's fast and hit us with, "You know, girls, the best things in life are free."

"Like money?" Isabella asked. "So, like, free money. Free money would be one of the best things in life, right?"

Isabella really excels at this sort of question, so her mom really excels at answering them.

"Go outside," she said.